THE EGG

BY

Geraldo Valério

OWLKIDS
BOOKS

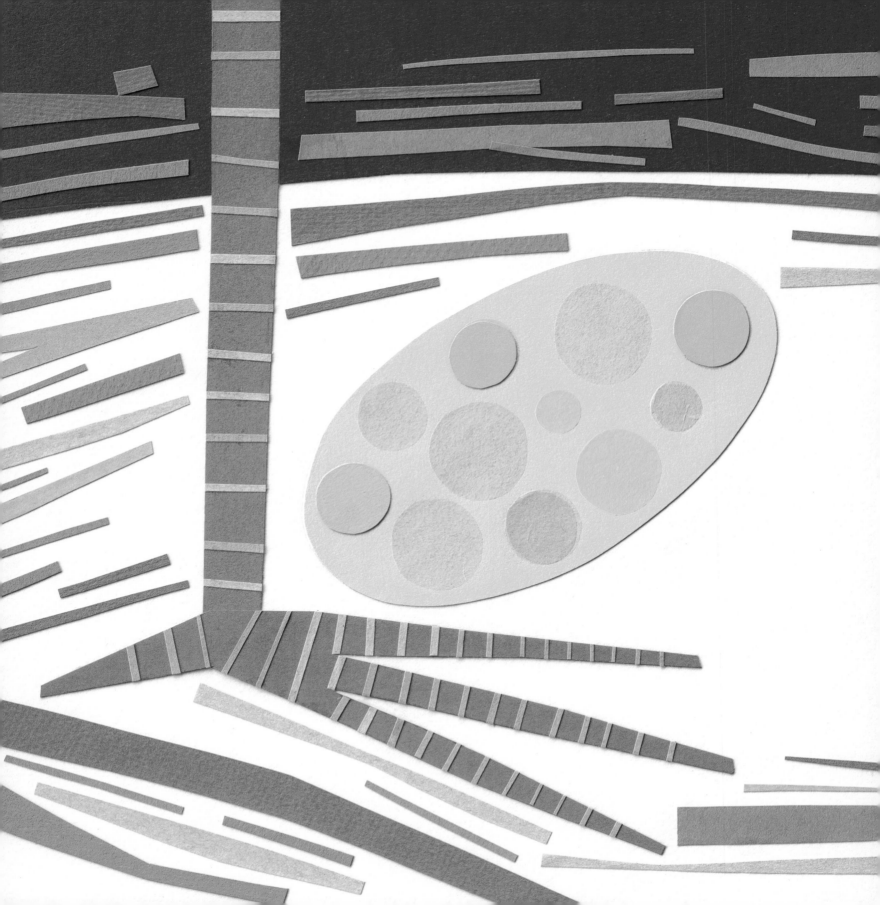

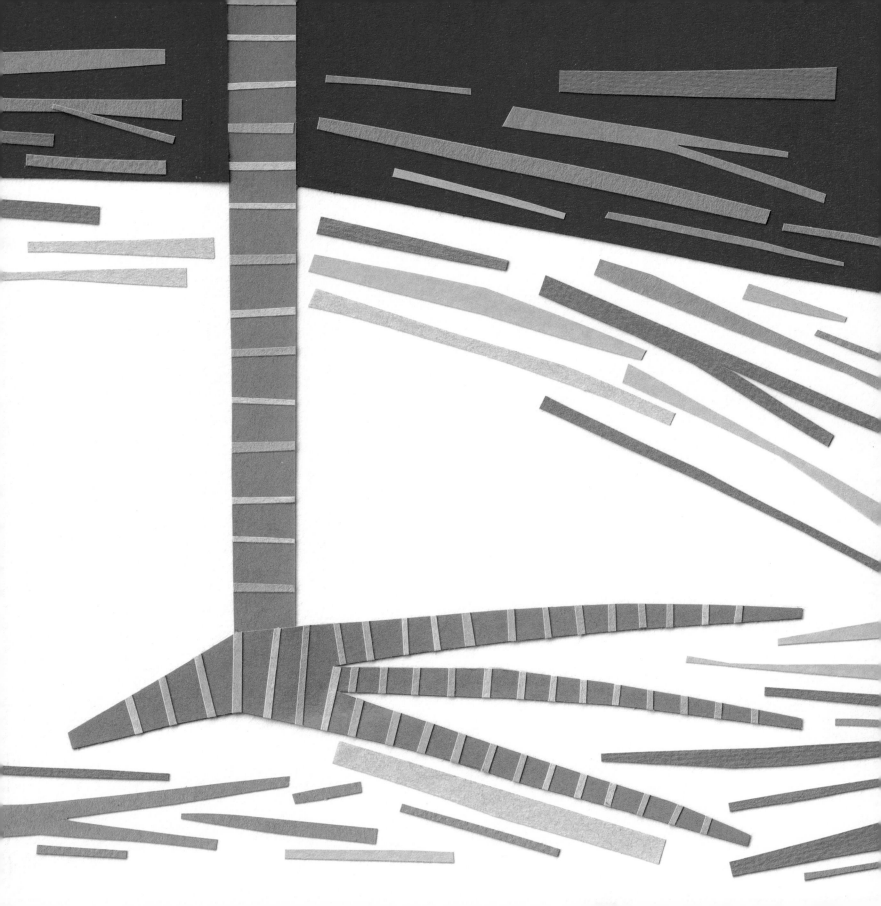

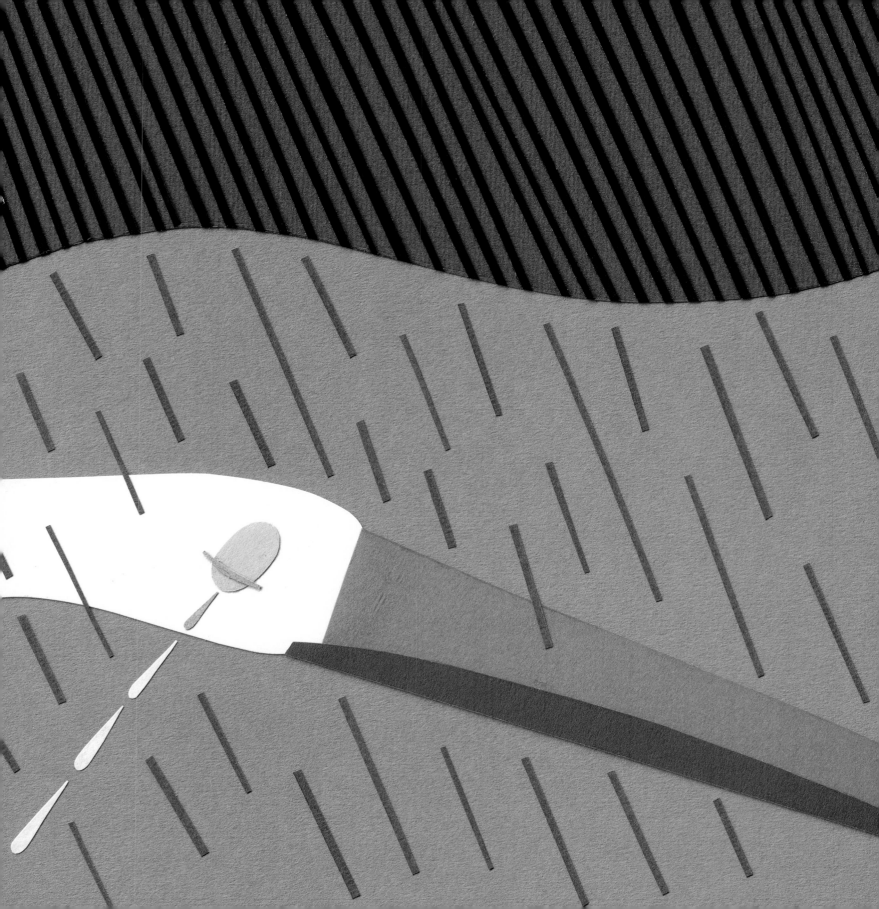

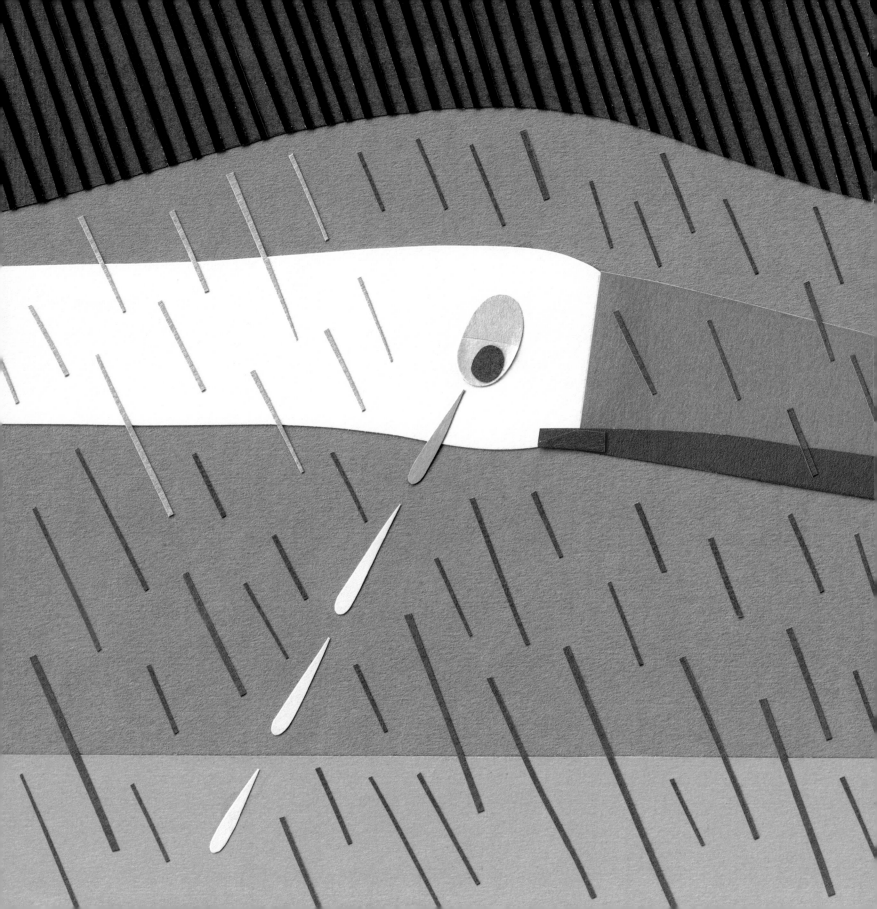

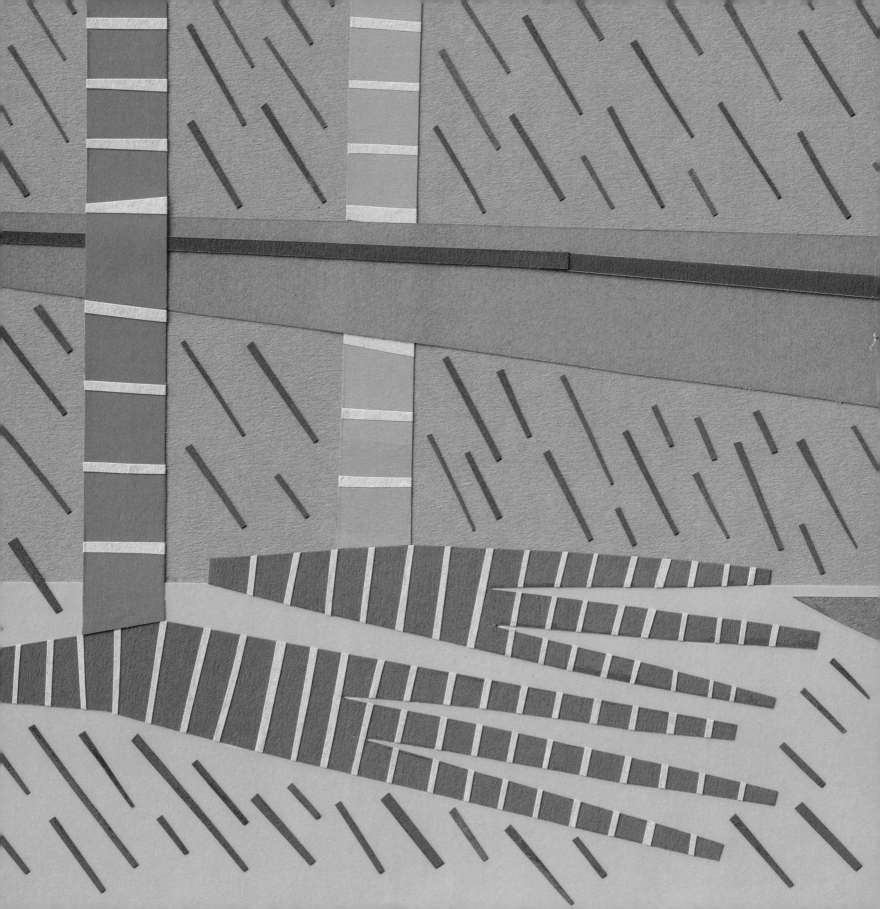

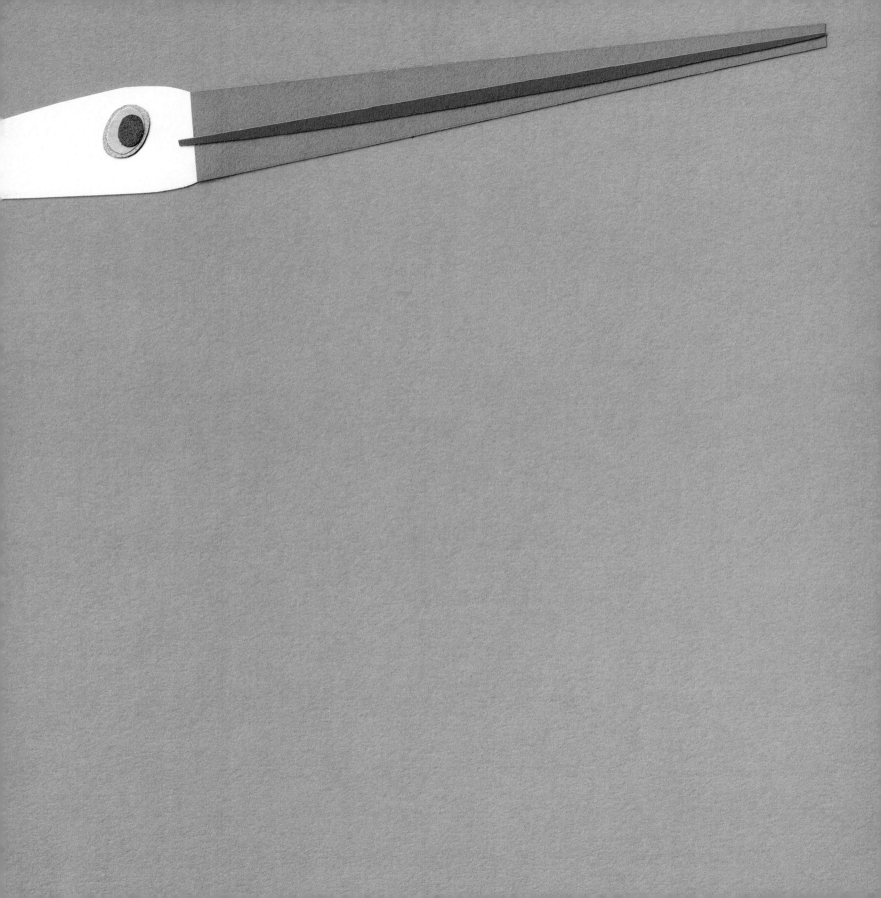

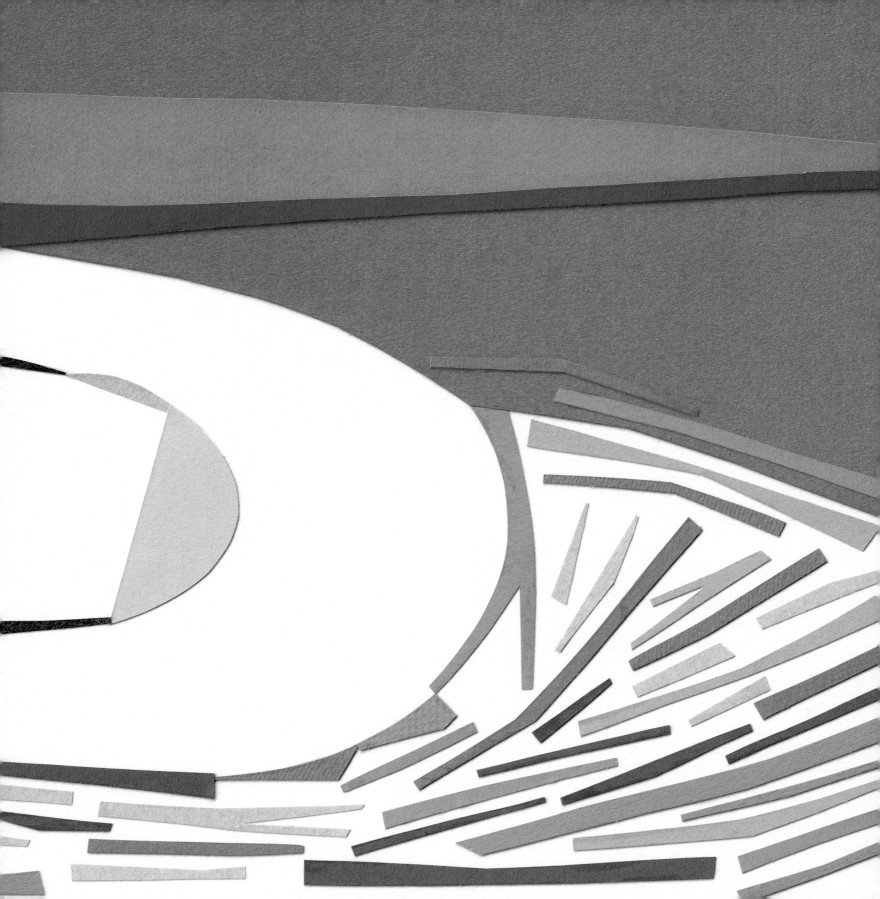

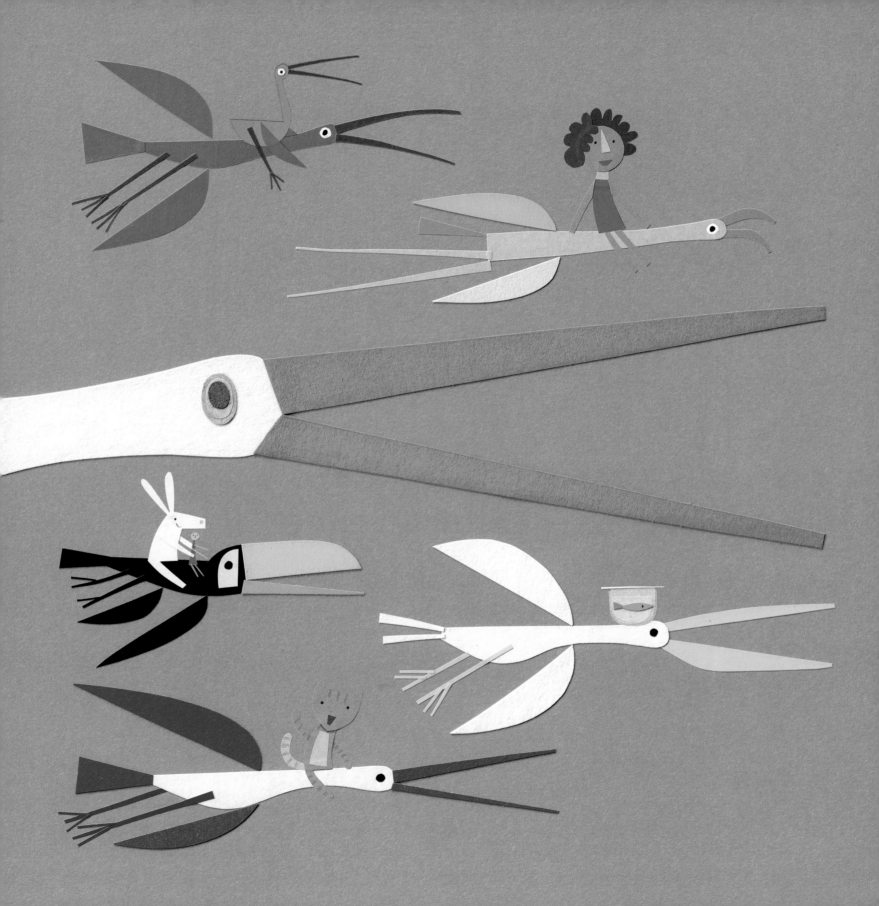

Owlkids Books acknowledges the financial support of the Canada Council for the Arts, the Ontario Arts Council, the Government of Canada through the Canada Book Fund (CBF) and the Government of Ontario through the Ontario Creates Book Initiative for our publishing activities.

Published in Canada by Owlkids Books Inc., 1 Eglinton Avenue East, Toronto, ON M4P 3A1
Published in the US by Owlkids Books Inc., 1700 Fourth Street, Berkeley, CA 94710

Library of Congress Control Number: 2019956170

Library and Archives Canada Cataloguing in Publication

Title: The egg / [written and illustrated] by Geraldo Valério.
Names: Valério, Geraldo, 1970- author, illustrator.
Identifiers: Canadiana 20190214538 | ISBN 9781771473743 (hardcover)
Classification: LCC PS8643.A422 E44 2020 | DDC jC813/.6—dc23

Edited by Debbie Rogosin | Designed by Alisa Baldwin

Manufactured in Shenzhen, Guangdong, China, in March 2020, by WKT Co. Ltd.
Job #19CB2383

A   B   C   D   E   F

Publisher of Chirp, Chickadee and OWL
www.owlkidsbooks.com

Owlkids Books is a division of bayard canada